# 1
# SCHOOL DINNER
# DISASTER

# THE
# SCHOOL DINNER
# DISASTER

*by*
JACQUELINE PINTO
*Illustrated by Trevor Stubley*

HAMISH HAMILTON
LONDON

First published in Great Britain 1983 by
Hamish Hamilton Children's Books
Garden House 57–59 Long Acre London WC2E 9JZ

Copyright © 1983 by Jacqueline Pinto
Illustrations copyright © 1983 Hamish Hamilton Ltd

British Library Cataloguing in Publication Data

Pinto, Jacqueline
    The school dinner disaster.—(Antelope books)
    I. Title
    823′ .914 [J]     PZ7

ISBN 0-241-11117 X

Filmset in Baskerville by
Katerprint Co Ltd, Cowley, Oxford
Printed in Great Britain at the
University Press, Cambridge

*For my family*

# Chapter 1

DARREN DRAKE was the first to hear the news. He had not actually meant to listen: he had just been walking past Mr Page's room when his feet suddenly seemed to stop. The door was open and Mr Page was talking to another man and waving his arms around in the special way that he did when he was angry.

Mr Page was the headmaster of Redwood Primary School. He was a short man and had an even shorter temper – except, of course, when parents were around. Darren saw that he had gone red in the face.

"I will not allow you to close down our school canteen!" shouted Mr Page. "Everyone here likes school dinners. Go and find another school which is spending too much money and leave us alone!"

Then Mr Page saw Darren standing open-mouthed outside his room. He glared at him and shut the door firmly in his face.

Within seconds Darren was out in the playground where the rest of the school were busy enjoying themselves. It was almost the end of lunch break so Darren had to work fast. He rushed round, "News!" he yelled. "Come over to the stump and I'll tell you what's happening!"

Darren jumped on the stump and waved his arms around – rather in the same way that Mr Page had done. In

3

fact, in more ways than one, Darren was like Mr Page. He was short, got cross quickly and was very good at telling everyone else what to do.

"Good news or bad news?" Jim asked Darren. Jim and Mike were Darren's special friends. "Are they going to close the school down?" To Jim, this would be good news – but not to Darren who thought Redwood was great in spite of the teachers.

"Worse than that!" shouted Darren. "They're going to close down the school canteen!"

"They *can't* do that!" said a scornful voice. Darren glared at Lucy Farmer. Trust her not to believe him! All the teachers liked Lucy because she worked so hard. Darren did not like her because she always argued with him.

"It's true, I tell you!" Darren shouted at Lucy. "Mr Page was yelling his head off to a man who was in his room. I didn't see who it was but he might have been from the Council. My dad saw in the local paper this morning that someone from the Council was going to visit all the schools in this area to see how they could save money."

"What will we do?" asked Sarah Moore in dismay. Her favourite lesson was cookery and school dinners made the whole day worth while. "We shall starve if we have to go all that time without food."

Darren stared at her scornfully. "We'll have to bring sandwiches instead."

At this, even Jim's smile faded. "It's not fair!" he grumbled. "School is the only place where we can have sausages and chips and jelly and ice cream EVERY day."

Mike's dad worked at the local factory and Mike knew a lot of things that the rest of Class Three did not. Slowly and thoughtfully he said. "We shall have to form a Committee and start a protest. We might have to call the whole school – and even the teachers – out on strike!"

Class Three stared admiringly at Mike. This was *brilliant!*

But Darren had his doubts. "Mr Page and Miss Wilson wouldn't strike. Can you imagine them leading us round the streets carrying banners? Still, having a Committee's not a bad idea. I'll be chairman, of course. Mike can be vice chairman and Jim can be treasurer. We could negotiate." (Darren's Dad worked at a big engineering firm so he also knew a thing or two about strikes and disputes.)

Jim was disappointed that Mike's idea had been dismissed so firmly. Then his grin came back. "I know! We could kidnap the man from the Council and keep him until he agrees to give us enough money to keep our canteen."

The others ignored him. Trust Jim to be silly when everyone else was deadly serious.

Mike had another idea. "If we could earn some money, it might be enough to save the canteen," he said slowly.

"Just what I think," agreed Darren at once. He was the chairman so he did not want Mike to have *all* the ideas.

9

Sarah looked doubtful. "How could we get enough money?" she demanded. "We would need thousands of pounds. I wouldn't give any of my pocket money. I need it all for sweets."

Darren was fed up with Sarah. "We only formed our Committee two minutes ago. Give us a chance to work things out. We shall have to talk it over."

"Not now, we won't!" said Mike, glancing at his watch. "Break is finished and we had better hurry up or Mr Page will start looking for us."

Mr Page was, as it happened, looking at them right this minute. He had been watching them from a class room window. "Darren and his lot are up to something," he said to Miss Wilson, his tall and trusty deputy head. "I can feel it in my bones."

Miss Wilson was used to Mr Page 'feeling things in his bones'. She always kept calm in crises, which was why Mr Page rushed to her the moment things went wrong. "Don't you worry," she said reassuringly. "I'll keep an eye on him. In fact," she went on as she watched Darren's wild gesticulations from the tree stump, "on this occasion, I shall keep both my eyes on him!"

## Chapter 2

DARREN AND CLASS THREE were not the only ones to be upset. The teachers did not want to give up school dinners either. They said they were far too busy to make themselves sandwiches every day.

Miss Wilson said briskly, "We must just put our heads together and see how we can save our school canteen."

Down in the kitchen, Mr Page was busy consoling the school cook. She was the most upset of them all. When she heard the news, she burst out crying and her tears went plop, plop, plop into the steaming pan of tomato soup.

Mr Page patted her on the shoulder. "Now calm down, Mrs Bragg. Of course I understand that you don't want to lose your job and we certainly don't want to lose your delicious school dinners. We are not going to give up our canteen without a struggle. The first thing we are going to do is to contact all the parents to hear their views."

That afternoon, just as school was about to end, Miss Wilson went into each form room to give out a pile of papers. When she got to Class Three, she handed a batch to Darren. "Pass these round, please, and don't forget, everyone, to give them to your parents. We are inviting them to a meeting in two weeks' time and we hope they will all come. Mr Robert Young, who is on the Schools' Committee of the local

Council, is going to talk to us about our canteen."

"Can we come, too?" asked Darren.

"Certainly not!" replied Miss Wilson sharply. "This meeting is only for parents!"

"That's all right," said Darren after Miss Wilson had left the room. "We have already had *our* meeting and ours was only for us. I think I had better find out more about Mr Young before we decide what to do next."

Finding out more about Mr Young proved easier than Darren had expected. At tea that day, Mrs Drake kept talking about a lady who had just come to live in one of the new houses on the Fairfield Estate. "She and her husband have moved down from Scotland because they want to be near his elderly parents. She came to the cake sale at the Women's Institute today," went on Mrs Drake. "She has two boys . . ."

"How old?" interrupted Darren with an interest which swiftly disappeared when his mother said the eldest was four and the youngest was only two.

"Her name is Susan Young and her husband is called Robert. He goes

round checking on schools for the local Council."

"That's the man I have been telling you about!" shouted Darren. "The one who is trying to stop us having school dinners."

"All right, I'm not deaf," said Mrs Drake as she put her hands over her ears. "He is only doing his job." She had at first agreed with Darren that the

Council should not close the school canteen but now she was not sure whose side she was on. She did not want to quarrel with the nice young mother who had just joined the W.I. "We are going to meet Mr Young at your school in two weeks' time so meanwhile we shall just have to wait and see."

Darren sighed. "Wait and see!" was what his Mum always said when she did not want to make up her mind.

"It would mean I would have to take sandwiches to school every day," said Darren warningly.

"That's all right," replied Mrs Drake, much to Darren's annoyance. "I *like* making sandwiches. Besides, you eat far too many chips and sausage rolls. I could give you healthy sandwiches with brown bread and you could have an apple or orange, which would be much better for you than all that ice cream you have on your jelly."

Darren could see he was not going to get much help from his Mum.

Then an alarming thought struck him. If the other mothers thought the same way, they would be *glad* to have the school canteen closed down.

Darren frowned. He must arrange a Committee meeting at once. Thank goodness tomorrow was Saturday. "Can I ring Mike and Jim, Mum?" he said. "It's urgent. It won't wait until Monday."

"Well, yes – if you're quick," said Mrs Drake.

Darren dialled Mike's number.

"We've got to meet tomorrow morning," said Darren as soon as he heard Mike's voice. "The situation is

*desperate*. Unless we earn enough money, the canteen will probably be closed in two weeks' time."

Mike agreed at once. "I'll fix it with Jim," he assured Darren. "He is coming round soon to show me his new bike. Perhaps we could all go car-washing."

"Right, then, see you tomorrow outside Baxter's at nine o'clock," said Darren.

If the three of them worked really hard, they might yet save the school canteen.

## Chapter 3

BAXTER'S, where the boys had arranged to meet, was just opposite Redwood Primary School. It was everyone's favourite shop – small, friendly and full of good things to eat and drink.

Normally, Darren, Mike and Jim would spend ages inside Baxter's, but not today. They had too much on their minds to waste time on trivialities.

They had all arrived on the dot of nine in their working clothes – shabby jeans and oldest sweatshirts. Their buckets were tied on to the handlebars of their bicycles. This was the first time

they had ever tried to earn money
washing cars.

Before they set off, Jim said, "I've

24

had an idea! Not just an ordinary idea like you two have but a brilliant one!"

Darren and Mike looked doubtful. Jim *never* had ideas that worked.

"I looked up Mr Young in the phone book," went on Jim. "There is an R. Young who lives at No. 3, The Drive, on the Fairfield Estate. Now, if we offer to help him *without* being paid, it will put him in a good mood. Then, when we ask him if we can keep our canteen, he is sure to agree."

Darren and Mike were not convinced. "Still, I suppose it is worth a try," said Darren doubtfully. "Come on, let's get going."

The three boys cycled down the hill towards the Fairfield Estate. Jim knew exactly where The Drive was and within five minutes they were at No. 3.

A tall, grey-haired man was working in the garden. "Is that Mr Young?" asked Mike as they all braked hard.

"I suppose so," replied Darren. "I didn't actually *see* him when he was in Mr Page's room. Let's ask him."

"Excuse me" called Darren. "Are you Mr Young?"

"That's right," answered the man,

glad to have a moment's rest from his digging. "What can I do for you?"

"Well, it's really what we can do for *you*," said Darren. "We thought we would go round helping people this morning. . ."

"We don't want to be paid," interrupted Jim. He wanted to make sure his plan was properly carried out.

Mr Young looked amazed. This was a nice change from the usual boys who called at his door expecting money for doing almost nothing. These three were a real credit to their parents and to their school. "Well," he said thoughtfully, "I could do with some help with the autumn digging. There is another spade over there so if two of you got on with that and the other one started the weeding, then I could do some pruning."

Mr Young was startled by the speed with which the boys went into action. They worked so hard that within an hour all the work was done. He got his wife to give them a large drink of orange squash and some biscuits and at that point Darren started talking about how much they liked their school dinners.

"I didn't like them when I was a boy," said Mr Young. "Stodgy food, lumpy custard, and goodness knows what else we were made to eat. You boys are lucky to have a canteen where you can choose what you want."

This seemed the right moment to come to the point. "That's *exactly* why we want to keep our school canteen," Mike said and went on pleadingly, "couldn't you possibly change your mind and not make us close it down?"

Mr Young stared at him. "I don't know what you are talking about," he said in a puzzled voice. "What has your school canteen got to do with me?"

"But . . . but . . . we heard you were going to close it down," stammered Jim. "You said you were Robert Young . . ."

Then the light dawned on Mr Young.

"I am *Richard* Young. You want my son, Robert. He works for the local Council. He and his wife and children have just moved in to Fairfield. They live across the road at No. 22."

The boys were aghast. They stood with their mouths wide open and looked such a strange sight that Mr Young couldn't help laughing. He dug his hand into his pocket and drew out a wallet. "Thank you, anyway, for helping me. I know you did not want any money but here is a five pound note. I expect you can find a use for it."

As they cycled away, some very rude words passed between Darren and Mike and Jim – the sort of words which would have made Mr Young change his mind about them being a credit to their parents and to their school.

Jim was quick to defend himself. "Well, it was your fault, too. You knew Mr Young had just moved in so you should have realized that he could not possibly be in the phone book yet."

"Oh, forget it!" growled Darren, who

was even more annoyed at this because he knew Jim was right.

They were just passing a large house, outside which was a white car spattered with mud. "Let's stop and see if we can clean that one," said Mike.

Within seconds, they were down the drive and at the front door. A smartly-dressed lady opened it and glared at them. "What do you want?" she demanded in a bad-tempered voice.

"We are earning money for our school canteen," explained Darren. "Can we clean your car?"

The lady frowned and shook her head. "Certainly not!" she said. "It's a brand new car and my husband wouldn't want scruffy boys clambering over it."

They were all indignant at this insult.

"We can't wear our best clothes

when we go car washing," said Darren crossly.

"I haven't got any best clothes," said Mike. "I wear jeans all the time. My Mum washes them every now and then. The ones I've got on were clean this morning."

"You car is much dirtier than we are!" said Jim.

The lady began to have second thoughts. Her husband would soon be home for lunch and they were going out immediately afterwards to visit one of his customers. She knew they would be in a great hurry if they were to arrive in time for the appointment. They certainly would not be able to go through the car wash. Perhaps she should let them do the car after all.

"Very well," she agreed reluctantly. "Now mind you take care. Don't

scratch the body-work and be sure to polish all the silver bits and don't leave any smears on the windows."

"Blimey!" muttered Darren as they went over to the outside tap to fill their buckets. "I'm sorry we came here. It will be a job to satisfy her!"

"Look, there's a hose!" said Jim, rushing forward to grab it first. "Let's hose the car and then we can polish it afterwards."

"Okay," agreed Mike as he and Darren fixed the other end of the hose to the outside tap.

"Right," called Jim. He twisted the spray end. This was going to be fun. Unlike the others, he was not used to cleaning cars. His Dad had a motor bike and you never used a hose on that. "Switch on!" he said.

Mike turned the tap on full.

The water shot out in a good, strong jet. Jim sprayed the back of the car, then came round to the side.

"Stop! Stop! Stop!" screamed Darren and Mike.

"Why?" asked Jim in surprise. "What am I doing wrong?"

"The windows are open, you idiot!" groaned Darren. "Look what you've done. You've soaked the inside of the car!"

Jim stared in horror at the puddles of water on the seats and on the floor.

Hearing their screams, the smartly-dressed lady came rushing out of the house. She saw at a glance what they had done.

"Oh no!" she cried. "How *could* you be so stupid!"

"We are sorry," said Darren feebly.

"I didn't realise the windows were

open," said Jim, explaining the obvious.

"We can probably dry it up with our sponges and dusters," said Mike, trying to be helpful.

"Don't you dare touch my car again!" shouted the lady, now almost beside herself with rage. "I shall have to get the gardener to clear up the mess you have made and that will cost me a lot of money! I shall tell your school about you and I shall tell your fathers and I shall tell. . ."

Darren was not chairman for nothing. Quick as a flash, he took control. "We will pay for the gardener to clean your car."

Before the lady had a chance to reply, Darren handed her the five pound note which Mr Young had given them. Then they turned sharply and ran up the drive. They jumped on their bikes and pedalled furiously down the road. They were out of sight before the lady had time to ask their names and addresses.

"Phew!" breathed Darren when at last they paused to rest. "Thank goodness we got away from her."

For a moment, even Jim looked dejected. "All that hard work for nothing!" he grumbled. Being treasurer was not proving much of a job.

"Oh, well," said Mike philosophically, "we shall just have to think of a different way to save the school canteen."

## Chapter 4

MR PAGE AND MISS WILSON, meanwhile, also had plans. They had invited Mr Robert Young and Miss Breedy from the Finance Department of the Council to come and taste the school dinners.

"We will get Mrs Bragg to put on one of her special meals," said Mr Page happily. "That will do the trick. Mr Young and Miss Breedy will enjoy it so much that they will have second thoughts about closing down our canteen."

Miss Wilson got out her notebook. "Right," she said in her bossy voice that Mr Page loved and Class Three hated. "We can start with Mrs Bragg's home-made tomato soup. We can have a bowl of cream on the table. We can each help ourselves to a large spoonful and stir it into our soup. After that, we can have some nice chicken mayonnaise with a salad. For dessert, I am sure they would enjoy our apple pancakes."

"That would be a lot of work for Mrs Bragg," said Mr Page thoughtfully. "Could she manage?"

"Yes, easily," replied Miss Wilson, who was looking forward to enjoying this extra special dinner herself. "Some of the girls from Class Three can help. Lucy Farmer and Sarah Moore would be best: Lucy Farmer is always quick and efficient and Sarah Moore likes cooking far more than school work. I will speak to them this afternoon and arrange everything."

Lucy and Sarah were delighted. As soon as Miss Wilson left the room, the rest of Class Three crowded round with plenty of advice.

Darren said in his best chairman's voice, "Be careful you don't spill the soup on them."

"You don't have to tell us that," replied Lucy crossly. "Miss Wilson wouldn't have asked us if she hadn't known that we would do it properly."

Sarah was jumping up and down with excitement. "I hope we can taste everything *before* we give them their dinner and then finish up anything that is left."

Next day Lucy and Sarah went into the kitchen shortly before the meal was due to be served. Mrs Bragg gave them each a white apron as well as so many instructions that the girls were not quite sure what they were supposed to be doing.

Mrs Bragg loved cooking and she loved having visitors but a special meal was always a worry. Mr Page had told her that a lot depended on this meal. She spent so much time and trouble with the preparations that when the moment came to serve the food she got herself into a real panic.

The table in Mr Page's room had been covered with a clean white cloth and the knives and spoons and forks had had a special rub-up for the occasion. There were even paper napkins and salt and pepper and some cans of beer.

When Mrs Bragg heard the ring of the bell from Mr Page's room, she collapsed on to her kitchen stool. "They're ready!" she screamed at Lucy

and Sarah. "Quick! Quick! Sarah, take the bowl of cream and put it on the table. Lucy, take the tray with the soup plates. Walk very slowly and be sure

47

not to spill it. Then come back and stir these pieces of cold chicken into the mayonnaise while I prepare the pancakes."

Lucy and Sarah did as Mrs Bragg said. Mr Page was at one end of the table, with Miss Wilson at the other.

Mr Young was sitting opposite the fat
and fussy-looking Miss Breedy.

They all smiled at Lucy and Sarah.
Miss Wilson said proudly, "The girls at
Redwood take a great interest in cookery and these are two of our best
pupils."

49

Sarah put the bowl of cream on the table and then helped Lucy with the plates of soup.

Mr Page said, "Mrs Bragg makes sure the school dinners are tasty and nourishing. All the boys and girls love her tomato soup – although they don't have cream!" he added with a a little laugh as he passed the bowl to Miss Breedy. "This is just for special occasions."

The visitors helped themselves. They each took a large dollop.

Miss Wilson started telling Miss Breedy and Mr Young how sorry the parents would be if the school canteen were closed down. "They know their children have such good food here."

To her amazement, fat and fussy Miss Breedy said, "Well, I can't say I agree. This soup is awful." She swal-

lowed a few more spoonfuls. "In fact, it is worse than awful. It is revolting!"

Mr Young pulled a face. "I must say," he murmured, "that I have never tasted tomato soup quite like this before."

Mr Page and Miss Wilson had been so busy talking that they hadn't yet started their soup. They stared at each other in amazement. They had not expected members of the Council to be so rude.

They both took a mouthful. Mr Page immediately spat his back into his soup plate. Miss Wilson more politely swallowed hers, then she clutched her stomach. "Oh, good heavens!" she said in alarm. "I think there has been some mistake. Please don't drink any more soup. We will go straight on to the chicken mayonnaise."

Lucy and Sarah took away the plates and then came back with the chicken.

Mr Young and Miss Breedy were now feeling hungry. They helped themselves to large portions of the second course and then started eating.

For a few moments, no one spoke. They just chewed and swallowed, chewed and swallowed.

Then Miss Breedy pushed her plate away. "This is even worse than the soup!" she declared. "If the boys and girls at Redwood have to eat food like this, I think the canteen should be closed immediately."

Mr Young said nothing but he, too, pushed his plate away.

Mr Page and Miss Wilson looked at each other in horror. They were both feeling distinctly queasy. What *had* Mrs Bragg done to the chicken.

For once, even Miss Wilson was lost for words. Miss Breedy's pink face was turning a faint shade of green. Then she stood up and rushed from the room. Mr Young followed her through the hall and outside into the fresh air. They stood for a few minutes taking deep breaths.

Mr Page and Miss Wilson remained

sitting at the table. They looked as
though they had been glued to their
seats.

Then Mrs Bragg came rushing in. She was on the verge of hysterics. "Those girls! Those girls!" she screamed. "They have ruined my meal. They have mixed up all the ingredients. The food must have tasted terrible."

"It did!" said Mr Page weakly.

"Where have the visitors gone?" wailed Mrs Bragg. "I can make them a nice omelette instead."

Mr Page went over to the window. He was just in time to see Mr Young and Miss Breedy disappearing into Baxter's. He shook his head sadly. "It is no good. We are too late. I am afraid they will never come here for dinner again."

## Chapter 5

DARREN AND THE OTHERS could hardly believe their ears when Lucy and Sarah crept back into the class room and told them what had happened.

"You mean to say that Mr Young and Miss Greedy. . . " began Darren.

"Breedy!" interrupted Lucy.

Darren gave her a withering glance. "You mean to say they were sick after eating their school dinner and. . ."

"Not quite," interrupted Lucy again. "At least not as far as we know. They only *felt* sick. They rushed out of Mr Page's room and he and Miss Wilson just sat there looking at each other.

Then Mrs Bragg started screaming at us so we got out of her way as quickly as we could."

"It wasn't our fault," said Sarah indignantly. "Mrs Bragg should have made sure that nothing got mixed up but she was in such a flap about her apple pancakes that we got in a muddle."

"Of *course* it was your fault!" said Darren in just the tone of voice that Mr Page would have used. "Didn't you taste it first?"

"How could we?" demanded Sarah. "There weren't any spoons near the dishes."

"You should have stuck your finger in and licked it," said Mike. "That is what *I* would have done."

Lucy and Sarah sighed.

Jim was disappointed. His job of

treasurer seemed to be a non-starter. "I suppose we shall have to give up and let them close down the canteen."

But Darren and Mike were not so easily defeated.

"We can't give up," declared Darren. "We shall have to think of something else."

Mike was silent for a moment. Now what would his father do if a crisis like this arose in the factory. "I know," he said slowly. "We must send a deputation . . ."

"A what?" asked Sarah, thinking that Mike might be planning to cook something really nice. A 'deputation' sounded like a lovely creamy pudding.

"A deputation is a group of people who go and see whoever is in charge when they want something special done. Now, if we all go and see Mr

Young next Sunday afternoon when he is sure to be home we could apologize for the disgusting meal that Lucy and Sarah gave him and we could ask him to get his Council to reconsider its decision." Mike paused for breath. He felt pleased with himself. He had got that out all right. Not many vice chairmen could explain things as well as that.

The others thought Mike's idea was great. They arranged to meet at ten thirty on Sunday morning outside Baxter's to make final plans for their visit to Mr Young.

"We shan't wait for you if you are late," said Darren sternly to Sarah and Lucy.

Sarah and Lucy glared but said nothing. Darren had been in a bad mood all day.

It was true that Darren was in a bad

mood. He felt hot and cross. He didn't
want any supper and didn't want to
watch television.

On Saturday morning he felt worse. Hotter and crosser and not wanting to bother about anything.

At breakfast, Mrs Drake gave him a bowl of cereal and some toast. "We are going to get you some new jeans and a tee shirt this morning and I don't want you to say you're hungry the moment we get there."

"I won't!" said Darren grumpily. "I don't want anything to eat and I don't want any new jeans. There's nothing wrong with my old jeans. I like them being too short and too tight and no one ever has new jeans."

Mrs Drake said soothingly, "Your new jeans won't look new for more than a week and you always like choosing tee shirts."

Darren sighed. He could see there was no point arguing.

A short while later, they were at Fairfield Stores. Darren leaned against the counter as his Mum picked up two pairs of jeans. She rummaged through a pile of shirts and pulled out three brightly-coloured ones. "What do you think of these?"

Darren hardly glanced at them. "You can choose," he said in a grouchy voice. "I don't like any of them."

Mrs Drake steered Darren to the fitting room. "Hurry up," she said. "The sooner we choose them, the sooner we'll be home."

Darren studied his face in the mirror. Except for a couple of spots on his forehead, he looked just as usual but he certainly did not feel it. His head hurt and his throat was dry and his back tickled. He pulled off his shirt.

Mrs Drake was just about to hand

one of the new shirts to him when she stopped. She peered at his face, then she looked at his back.

Quickly, she put Darren's old shirt

back on him, then grabbed his hand and hurried him from the changing room.

Just then an assistant came by. "I have found some more shirts. Would your son like any of these?"

Mrs Drake seemed completely flustered. "No, thank you," she said quickly. "I have changed my mind. We won't buy anything today. Sorry to have bothered you. Goodbye and thank you."

Darren could not make things out. One minute his Mum wanted him to have new clothes, the next minute she didn't!

Still holding Darren's hand, Mrs Drake rushed out of the shop. "We must get home at once," she said. She walked along so briskly that Darren almost had to run to keep up with her.

As soon as they were inside their house, Mrs Drake put her hand on his forehead. "Goodness, you feel hot! I had better take your temperature."

Then things happened very quickly. In next to no time, Darren was tucked up in bed between nice cool sheets. His mother fussed round him, banging up his pillow to make him more comfortable and bringing him a large mug of blackcurrant juice.

"You have got chicken pox," announced Mrs Drake. She used to be a nurse so she knew just what those spots meant. "The moment you took your shirt off in the shop, I realized that was what had been making you so cross. Your back is covered with spots!"

"Oh, no," Darren groaned. "I can't have chicken pox . . . not this weekend, anyway. I've got to be at Baxter's tomorrow morning at ten thirty."

"The only place you will be tomor-row morning is right here in bed!" said Mrs Drake firmly. "Whatever you planned to do will just have to wait."

## Chapter 6

WHEN HE WOKE UP next day, Darren was tickling all over. He pulled up the sleeves of his pyjamas and saw masses of red blobs.

By the time Mrs Drake came bustling in with his breakfast tray, Darren was feeling very sorry for himself. Here he was stuck in bed with chicken pox when he should be out with the others trying to save the school canteen. "Are you sure I can't get up?" he pleaded. "Mike and I have something very important to do with Jim and Sarah and Lucy."

Mrs Drake shook her head. "Mike won't be doing anything today. He is in bed too. His mother has just phoned to say he has chicken pox so Jim and the girls will have to manage without you both."

Darren scowled. Jim and the girls were absolutely no use by themselves. They never had good ideas of their own.

He lay back in bed and sighed. By the time he and Mike were up and about again, the Council would have gone ahead and closed the canteen. He felt so cross and miserable that he could not eat his breakfast.

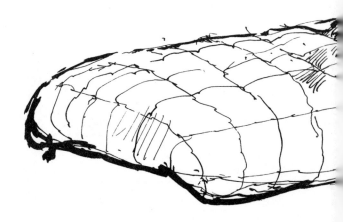

At ten o'clock, the door bell rang. Darren heard Jim's voice. He had decided to call for Darren on the way to Baxter's.

When Mrs Drake told him that both Darren and Mike had chicken pox, Jim was horrified. He was about to go back home when he remembered they had arranged to meet the girls.

"There is no point in doing anything without Darren and Mike," he told Mrs Drake in a disappointed voice. "I will just have to let Sarah and Lucy know that all our plans are cancelled."

Slowly and reluctantly, Jim trudged along the road to Baxter's.

Lucy and Sarah greeted him impatiently.

"Of course we can think of something to do," said Lucy scornfully when Jim said they might as well give up. "You can give up if you like but Sarah and I certainly won't."

"Then neither shall I," said Jim firmly. "But what *can* we do?"

Sarah said, "First of all, I must buy some chocolate. I want to make some crispy biscuits. I won't be a minute." She dashed into Baxter's and Lucy followed her.

While Jim waited outside, he thought of Sarah's crispy biscuits. She often made them and brought them to school and they were really good.

Then an idea came to him. Not the silly sort of idea he usually had – the sort that was meant to make the others laugh – but a really brilliant, sensible idea.

By the time Lucy and Sarah came out of the shop, Jim had it all worked out. "Listen!" he said. "If Sarah makes

some crispy biscuits, we can give them
to Mr Young as a present. When he has
eaten them, he will be very pleased with
us. Then we can ask him to persuade
the Council to let us keep our canteen."

Lucy and Sarah thought carefully for
a moment. Then they agreed.

They rushed back to Sarah's house.
Jim and Lucy watched while Sarah

made the biscuits. It didn't take long before they were cooked and could be tested. They tasted delicious.

They could hardly wait for the afternoon to come when they would go together to Mr Young's house. Jim and Lucy hurried home for lunch and agreed to meet again outside Baxter's at three o'clock.

This time they were determined nothing should go wrong. Sarah had put the chocolate crispy biscuits into a pretty tin her mother had found and she carried them carefully so they would arrive in perfect condition.

At first things went just as they planned. They hurried down the hill to the Fairfield Estate and made sure they were at No. 22 The Drive before they rang the bell. Mrs Young opened the door.

"We are from Redwood Primary School and we have brought a present for Mr Young," explained Jim importantly.

"I made it," said Sarah proudly.

"That's very kind of you," replied Mrs Young warily. She remembered what happened the last time her

husband ate Redwood School cooking. "Come through into the garden."

Mr Young was lying back in his sun-bed while his two young sons were trying to tip him up. He had just finished mowing the lawn and he was looking forward to his tea.

He looked surprised when he saw Jim and Sarah and Lucy trooping out of his house. He recognized the girls immediately. How could he ever forget them!

"Hello!" he said. "How are the Redwood school cooks? Tell me, do you often mix things up in the kitchen?"

"It has never happened before," answered Jim. "Mrs Bragg always makes super dinners."

"It was just a mistake!" said Lucy, indignantly.

Sarah came forward and handed over

the present. "Here are some special biscuits to make up for that awful dinner we gave you."

Mr Young opened the box, gave a biscuit to his wife and took one himself. "Umm," he said appreciately. "These are delicious . . . in fact they are the best chocolate biscuits I have ever had!"

His two sons wanted to taste them too. Mr Young gave them each one, and after a couple of minutes, they clamoured for another . . . and another!

Lucy then put on her most appealing voice. "When the Council has its meeting about our canteen, *please, please* will you get it to change its mind?"

Mr Young shook his head. "It had its meeting last Friday. It has already taken a decision about your school canteen. It will not change its mind now."

There was a stunned silence. Lucy was too furious to speak. Sarah stared down at the ground trying not to cry. What a waste to have given him her lovely chocolate biscuits.

Jim, too, was speechless. He was the most upset of them all. He wanted, more than anything in the world, to have an idea that really worked!

What made things even worse was that Mr Young suddenly laughed and said, "Cheer up!"

"How can we?" demanded Jim gloomily. "We shall have to eat boring sandwiches every day just because the Council is going to close down our canteen."

"I never said that!" replied Mr Young with a broad smile on his face.

Jim and Lucy and Sarah stared at him.

"You said the Council had taken a decision about our canteen," said Jim accusingly. "I heard you. Didn't he say that?" he asked, turning to the girls.

"Yes!" agreed Sarah and Lucy angrily. "You definitely said it had taken a decision."

"Ah," said Mr Young, still smiling. "But you didn't ask me what that decision was!"

"What do you mean?" said Jim hoarsely, hardly daring to hope.

"In view of my report that Redwood's school canteen is so popular with the boys and girls and the staff and parents, the Council has decided that it certainly should *not* be closed down."

The expression of utter gloom on Jim's face changed into a huge grin. Sarah and Lucy jumped up in the air with excitement. Mr Young handed

round the remaining chocolate biscuits
while Mrs Young opened a large bottle
of coke to celebrate.

On the way home, Jim and Sarah and
Lucy called at Darren's house.

Mrs Drake said Darren was still in
bed but Darren heard their voices and

came to the top of the stairs to listen.

"We went to see Mr Young," burst out Jim to Mrs Drake.

"The Council has changed its mind," added Lucy.

"We are going to keep our canteen," said Sarah excitedly.

Darren was flabbergasted. "How did you manage that?" he called down.

Mrs Drake spun round. "Get back to bed!" she ordered. "You have got a temperature!"

"Yes, get back to bed," echoed Sarah and Lucy annoyingly.

"What happened?" demanded Darren, but when he saw the expression on his mother's face he quickly went back to bed without waiting for a reply.

Jim and the girls exchanged glances. Without even speaking, they each knew what the other was thinking . . . of course, they would tell Darren what happened at Mr Young's – but not today. First they would spread the good news around and get everyone wondering why the canteen was to be saved – and how they had managed to do it!